The RAINBOW ZEBRA in the Land of the LuLee Ponies

Diane Elizabeth Kelleher

AuthorHouse™
1663 Liberty Drive
Bloomington, IN 47403
www.authorhouse.com
Phone: 833-262-8899

Because of the dynamic nature of the Internet, any web addresses or
links contained in this book may have changed since publication and
may no longer be valid. The views expressed in this work are solely those
of the author and do not necessarily reflect the views of the publisher,
and the publisher hereby disclaims any responsibility for them.

This book is printed on acid-free paper.

ISBN: 979-8-8230-2925-4 (sc)
ISBN: 979-8-8230-2926-1 (e)

Library of Congress Control Number: 2024924425

Print information available on the last page.

Published by AuthorHouse 01/21/2025

authorHOUSE®

The Rainbow Zebra in the Land of the LuLee Ponies

By Diane Elizabeth Kelleher

Now, because of their solid colors,
And their lack of black and white stripes,
And because each wore a jeweled crown,
Testimony to their personal renown,
The LuLee ponies believed
This and nothing other-
That they were the superior team-
A team more important than their neighboring zebras
With their stripes of stark black and white.

[Pronounced LouLee]

With each LuLee pony being only one colorful tone,
Of red or blue, yellow, green, or white,
The LuLee ponies now thought with all their might
That the entire meadow was THEIRS alone.

Now, although the LuLee ponies for many a decade
Had shared their grassy knolls and meadows,
In an arrangement rather uneasy,
With their neighborly herd of zebras,

Upon occasion and without a word,
the two equine herds
Sparred over the rights to own,
This resource that gave them life,
The field's long, lush shafts of fragrant grass of green
This meadow that sustained both
Of the opposing equine teams.

So, not very long ago,
But indeed far, far away,
One day, as if by heavenly magic,
Something special was seen to lay,
Born amidst the wavering hay,
In the land of the LuLee ponies.
A baby zebra was born,
Who was like no other ever seen before.
The baby zebra wasn' t like all the others.
It was not even like its own Mother.

Yes, the baby zebra's stripes were like no others'
In that they were composed of something unknown.
The baby zebra's stripes were not the expected
black and white,
Nor was the baby zebra altogether without any stripes.-

Instead, the baby zebra's stripes
Were composed of every imaginable color,
Every color of the heavenly rainbow,
Every color except black and white.

And when the team of zebras
Invited the LuLee ponies
Over to see the miracle of
The little rainbow colored zebra
In all of its mystery,
Something mystical happened.

All the LuLee ponies began to see
The zebras in an entirely
New and different sort of light.

In the presence of this wonderful new existence,
The LuLee ponies began to believe,
That they might have been wrong all along
About their neighborly zebras.

So, the leader of the LuLee ponies
Sang loudly out for everyone to hear:
"Now, I see very clearly-
The zebras are all just as good as are we..."

And all the zebras, black and white,
And the rainbow-striped zebra-baby,
Nodded to show that they agreed.

And so, from then on, there were no opposing teams.

Now, each and all wore a crown,

true testimony to each-and-all's new renown,

And everyone grazed in the meadow,

Together in peace and harmony,

As all the entities involved became one, big, happy family,

Sharing the entire bounty

Of the newly minted, true good will,

And life-saving grasses of green on the hill,

About the Author

Born and educated in Massachusetts, Miss Kelleher began her undergraduate studies in the Liberal Arts at prestigious Wheaton College in Norton, where she was on the Dean's List. A transfer student, she received the degree of "Bachelor of Arts with Distinction" from Simmons College (now Simmons University) in Boston. Graduating in the top five percent of her class while majoring in Sociology, Economics and Art History, beyond "Distinction" additional honors conferred included: Academy (Collegiate Honor Society), Departmental Recognition (History of Art), Dean's List and receipt of academic grants.

Further general art historical studies and specialized new directions reflecting a burgeoning interest in American Art and Culture, as well as European Painting of the Nineteenth Century, were undertaken within the Department of the History of Art, Master of Arts and Doctor of Philosophy program at Boston University's Graduate School of Arts and Sciences. By age twenty-four, she had independently researched and authored her first book and the first art historical book ever written on Boston artist, Lilian Westcott Hale – titled Enchantment: The Art and Life of Lilian Westcott Hale, America's Linear Impressionist. A year later came the independently researched and written Unlikely Icon: The Art, Culture and Philosophy of Forest Hills Cemetery, Boston: A Nineteenth Century Symbol of American Values and the majority of Sense, Sensibility and Sensation: The Marvelous Miniatures and Perfect Pastels of Laura Coombs Hills, America's Lyrical Impressionist.

Eventually, new interests in English literature beckoned, so Kelleher completed a Master of Arts Degree in English Literature at Clark University in Worcester, Massachusetts, where she received a full scholarship and wrote her book The Rose Upon The Trellis: William Faulkner's Lena Grove.

Currently enrolled in the Master of Science Degree in Business Administration at Worcester State University's graduate school, Kelleher is now finishing the last of the required business courses. Kelleher was also accepted to study at Clark University for the degree of Master of Business Administration, having been offered the Clark Alumni Scholarship of twenty-five thousand dollars.

A list of her other books appear on the following page. Kelleher is the niece of renowned Hollywood writer and producer, the late Paul W. Keyes of Paul W. Keyes Productions, Westlake Village, California.

DIANE ELIZABETH KELLEHER
ANNOUNCES THE AVAILABILITY OF HER BOOKS -

Sense, Sensibility, and Sensation:
The Marvelous Miniatures and Perfect Pastels
of Laura Coombs Hills,
America's Lyrical Impressionist

Enchantment: The Art and Life of Lilian Westcott Hale,
America's Linear Impressionist

Unlikely Icon: The Art, Culture and Philosophy of
Forest Hills Cemetery, Boston:
A Nineteenth Century Symbol of American Values

The Rose Upon the Trellis: William Faulkner's Lena Grove

How to Research, Write and Publish
An Art History Book in American Art

The Secrets of Willow Creek

The Fantasmagorical Feline Adventures of Little Miss Libby

Friendship Cottage: The Little House That Big Jack Built (A true story)

Lizzie and the Shelter Kitty (A true story) & Skippy Saves the Day

The Rainbow Zebra in the Land of the Lulee Ponies

From:
Author House
1663 Liberty Drive, Suite 200
Bloomington, IN 47403
1-800-839-8640 OR 1-888-519-5121
www.authorhouse.com
www.amazon.com
www.barnesandnoble.com

Printed in the United States
by Baker & Taylor Publisher Services